HOMEWORK

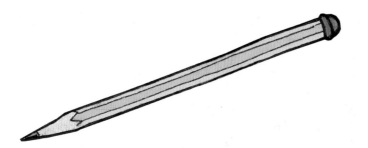

HOMEWORK

Arthur Yorinks

illustrated by

Richard Egielski

Walker & Company
New York

"Tony! Do your homework!"

First published in the United States of America in 2009 by Walker Publishing Company, Inc.
Visit Walker & Company's Web site at www.walkeryoungreaders.com

For information about permission to reproduce selections from this book, write to
Permissions, Walker & Company, 175 Fifth Avenue, New York, New York 10010

Library of Congress Cataloging-in-Publication Data
Yorinks, Arthur.
Homework / Arthur Yorinks ; illustrations by Richard Egielski.
p.   cm.
Summary: When Tony's pens, pencil, and eraser come to life, the squabbling set of writing
tools tries to complete Tony's neglected homework.
ISBN-13: 978-0-8027-9585-4 • ISBN-10: 0-8027-9585-4 (hardcover)
ISBN-13: 978-0-8027-9586-1 • ISBN-10: 0-8027-9586-2 (reinforced)
[1. Homework—Fiction. 2. Writing—Materials and instruments—Fiction.]
I. Egielski, Richard, ill. II. Title.
PZ7.Y819Ho 2009   [E]—dc22   2008028011

Art created with ink pens and watercolor on paper
Typeset in Garth Graphic
Book design by Nicole Gastonguay

Printed in China by Printplus Limited
(hardcover) 10 9 8 7 6 5 4 3 2 1
(reinforced) 10 9 8 7 6 5 4 3 2 1

All papers used by Walker & Company are natural, recyclable products
made from wood grown in well-managed forests. The manufacturing processes
conform to the environmental regulations of the country of origin.

For Ania, Nettie, Elka, and Art Brown IPS —A. Y.

To Mr. Kit —R. E.

One night, like almost every night, Tony's mom yelled, "Tony! Do your homework!" And like almost every night, Tony didn't do his homework. Instead, he sat on his bed, read a comic book, and then fell fast asleep.

But wait! On this particular night, something extraordinary happened. Wow, did it happen.

As Tony slept, his favorite #1 pencil decided to do Tony's homework. It hopped over to a fresh piece of paper and began to write a story:

Once upon a time,

Suddenly Tony's eraser called out, "That stinks!" and then erased the whole thing.

"What do you mean it stinks?" asked the pencil.

"Can't you speak English? It stinks!" said the eraser. "Stinkeroo!"

"But—," the pencil began.

"Do you want to get the kid an F?" continued the eraser. "Listen. *A long time ago* is a much better way to start.

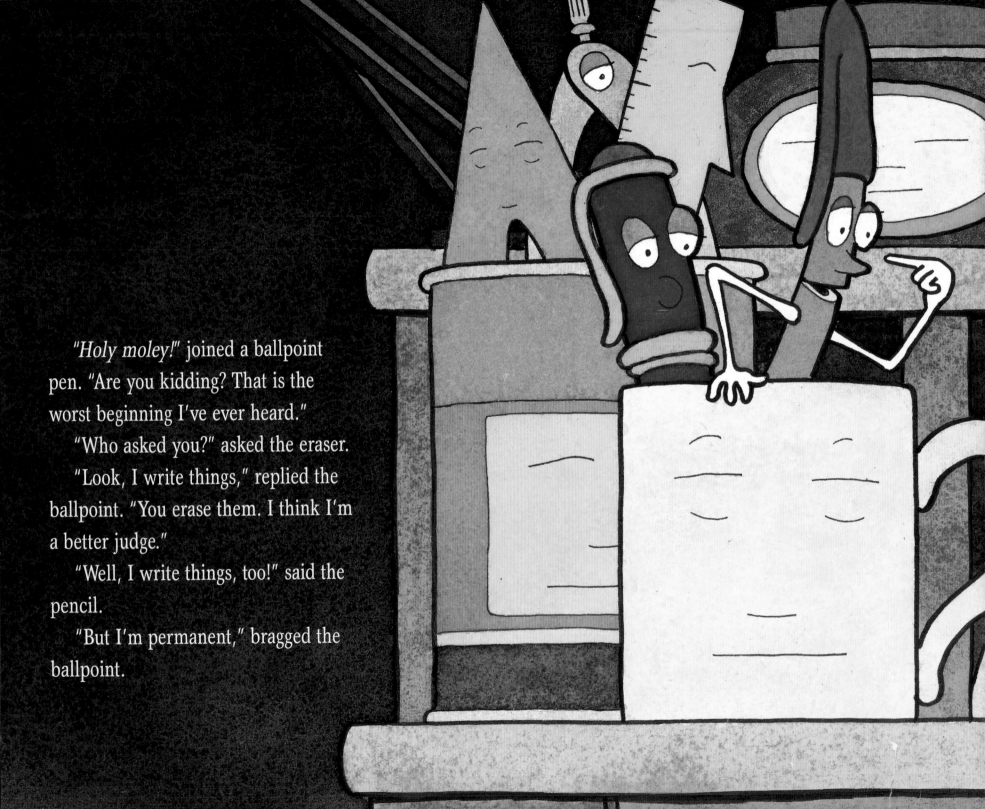

"*Holy moley!*" joined a ballpoint pen. "Are you kidding? That is the worst beginning I've ever heard."

"Who asked you?" asked the eraser.

"Look, I write things," replied the ballpoint. "You erase them. I think I'm a better judge."

"Well, I write things, too!" said the pencil.

"But I'm permanent," bragged the ballpoint.

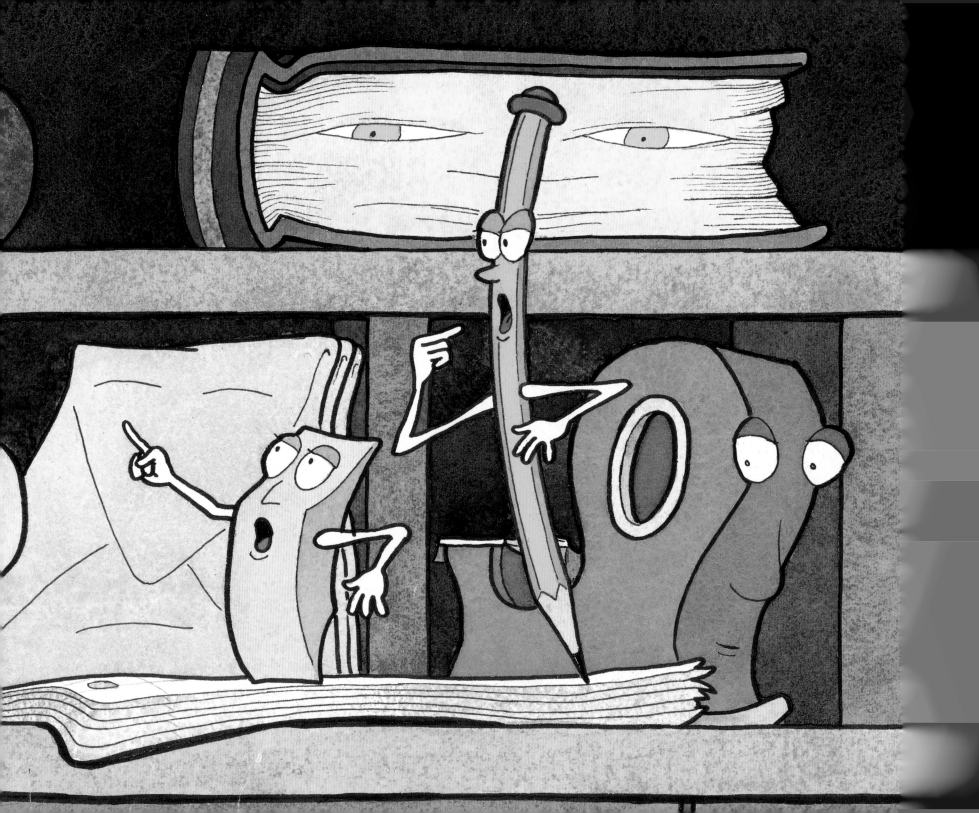

"Permanent?" yelled a fountain pen. It jumped onto the paper and made a big ink splotch. "*That's* permanent."

"What a jerk," said the eraser. "What are we supposed to do with this stupid splotch?"

"Splotch? That's no splotch," said the fountain pen. "That's art!"

"Look, you nincompoops," said the pencil. "The kid has to hand this in tomorrow, and all you can do is argue? Here, let me see if I can fix this."

The pencil wrote next to the big ink stain:

Once, there was a splotch. A big, fat splotch.

"Hmm, maybe you've got something," said the ballpoint.

"I don't know," said the eraser. "I think it may stink."

The fountain pen was very excited. Like a nutcase, it started making splotches all over the paper.

"All right!" said the ballpoint. "Now we're getting somewhere."

"You maniac!" cried the pencil. "You ruined it. My story is ruined!"

"What? What did I do?" asked the fountain pen.

"You splotched all over the place," said the ballpoint. "And now Tony's in big trouble."

"Big trouble," said the eraser.

"Maybe I can think of something," said the pencil. "Let me think." The pencil went over to the paper to write, then stepped back to think some more.

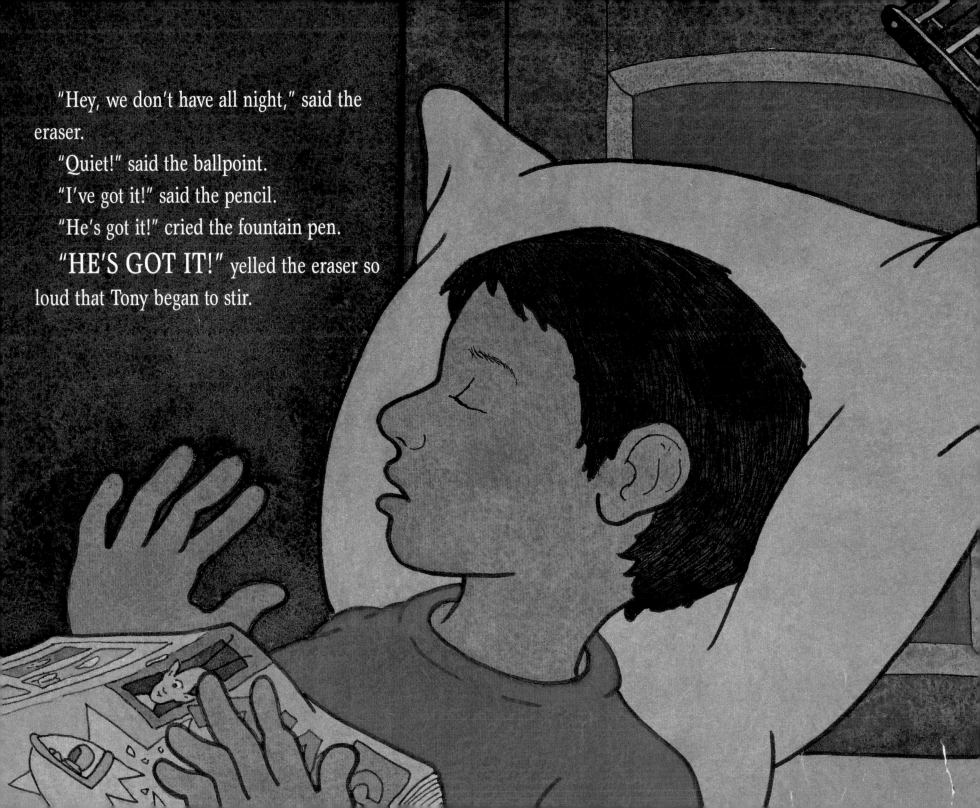

"Hey, we don't have all night," said the eraser.

"Quiet!" said the ballpoint.

"I've got it!" said the pencil.

"He's got it!" cried the fountain pen.

"HE'S GOT IT!" yelled the eraser so loud that Tony began to stir.

"Quick, hurry—before he wakes up," said the
ballpoint.
The pencil furiously began to write:

The Story of Planet Splotch
"Look! Captain Armstrong! We've landed on the
planet Splotch! We're surrounded by splotches!"

"Back to the ship, men!" declared the captain.

"But, sir, our ship's engines were destroyed when we landed."

The captain spoke. "I guess we'll have to make friends with the splotches. Be alert. One is coming now . . .

"Hello, Splotch. My name is Captain Armstrong."

The captain continued. "We come in peace. We—we—UGH! Help! I'm being eaten by a splotch. Run for your lives!"

It was no use. The splotches were mean splotches and the planet Splotch was no place for human life.

From that day on, spaceships from Earth never landed on the planet Splotch ever again.

THE END.

The pencil stopped writing and took a breath.
Everyone looked over and read. There was total silence.

"It's brilliant!" piped up the fountain pen. "It brought me to tears."

"Genius," said the ballpoint.

"IT'S THE BEST THING I'VE EVER READ!" yelled the eraser. **"I WOULDN'T ERASE ONE THING!"** The eraser yelled so loud that Tony woke up.

"Quick, hide!" whispered the pencil as everyone scattered.

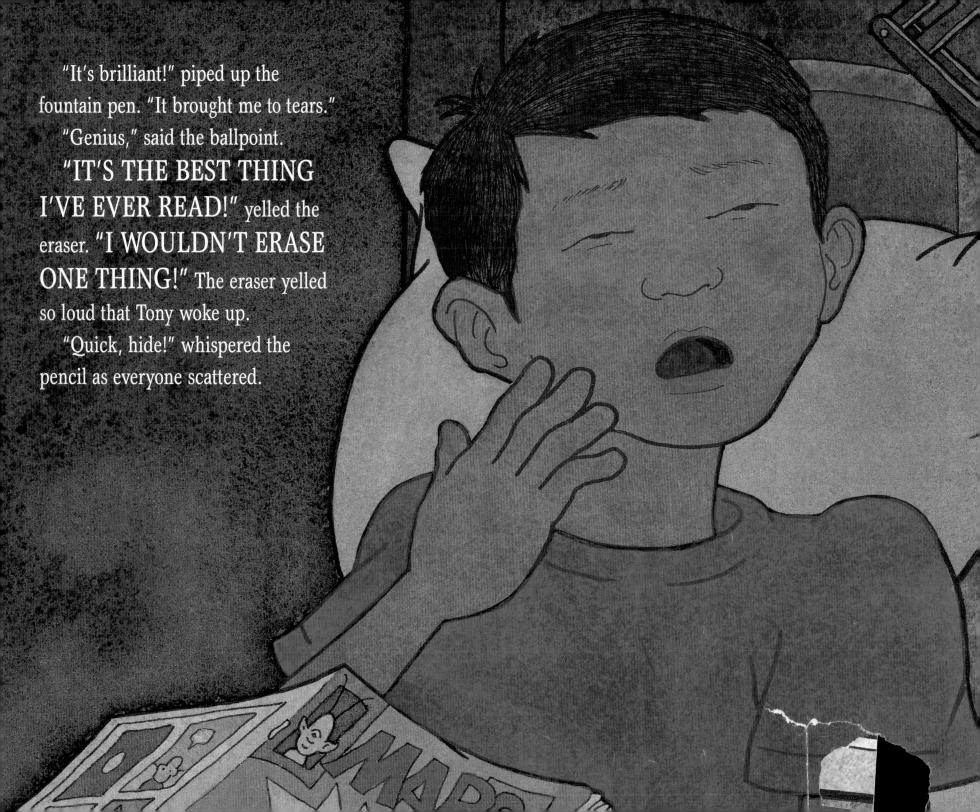

Tony went over to his desk, picked up the paper, and began to read. He had no idea where this story came from and, well, with all the splotches and crossed-out words, he just crumpled it up and threw it right into the garbage.

"Oh, what does he know?" whispered the eraser.

"The boy has no taste. He doesn't know what's good," said the fountain pen.

"At least we woke him up," murmured the ballpoint.

"Excuse me," said the eraser. "I think *I* was the one who woke him up."

Tony grabbed his pencil.

"Hey, he's starting over," whispered the eraser.

"Pencil!" said the ballpoint. "Don't do it! Don't write anything. We'll show him!"

"I can't help it," cried the pencil. "He's got me!"

"What's he writing?" asked the fountain pen.

"I can't see," said the eraser.

"It's a story," said the pencil after Tony finished and had left the room. "It's called *Life on Planet Splotch*."

"What!" said the ballpoint. "He stole our idea?"

"What do you mean *our* idea?" said the pencil. "It was *my* idea."

"Your idea!" said the fountain pen. "I suppose *you* made all the splotches—"

"Splotches? We didn't need any stinkeroo splotches," said the eraser.

"Oh, yeah!" cried the fountain pen. And the pencil and the eraser and both pens argued for the rest of the night—this rare night—when Tony, for once, did his homework.

And he even got a B.

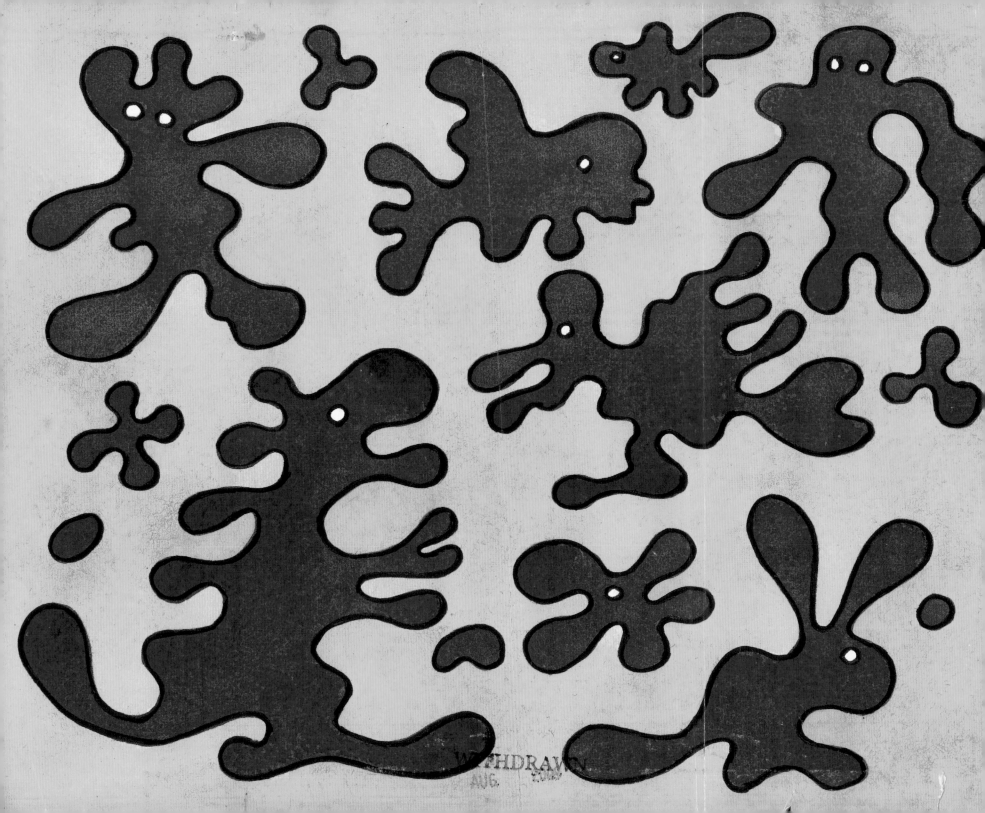